the MOON is out

by
Danielle Atherton-Rutledge

Illustrated by
Courtney Heinzmann Kamm

Memories,
magic
and morals
are made
at story time.

ALLISON, NOLAN, & MIA,
I love you to the moon and back.

The *moon* is out,

my little sprout.

I hope you ate your sauerkraut and peas
and asked for more, "please?"

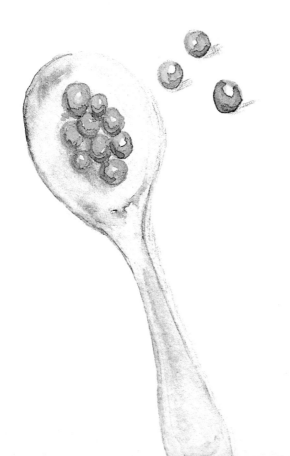

I hope you felt the
sunshine, breeze, raindrops,
or snow flurries *kiss*
the apples of your cheeks.

I pray you danced in a creek,

climbed a small mountain peak,

hit a ball off a golf tee,

gave someone a reason to smile for a week,

or maybe even *learned*

a new Spanish or Greek word like,

"Sobremesa" or "Ataraxia"

on this magnifico dia.

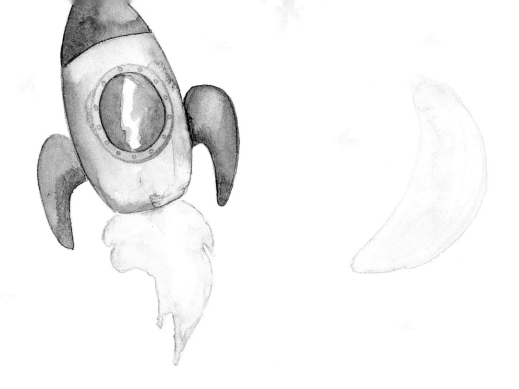

I wish for you to be
in your warm and cozy *pajamas*
while practicing your pranayama
instead of reflecting on any drama
or mistakes made
as you lay your sweet, soft cheeks
on your clean, crinkled pillows and sheets.

And I have *faith* that you will
gaze up before you rest up
with clasped hands and twinkling
eyes to say "thank you," and "hi," to
the moon and the stars
that light up the night sky.

Look up and inhale the *brilliance.*

know that you are a star—one in a billion.

Count back from ten to one
and exhale the entire day, it is done.

Tomorrow is a new one, a new day, new chances; but for now you may dance and sing in your dreams as the Moonbeams glisten and bestow their *blessings* on all that is below.

Now *close* your eyes, let go,
and know that all is
healthy, happy, and whole.

Sleep sweetly as you
sew your dreams
under the moon's soft glow.

Have you ever?

Have you ever sat in the sunshine and ate fermented cabbage called **sauerkraut** on your hot dog, brat, or salad? Then you have enjoyed a century-old German delicacy rich in vitamins and nutrients.

Have you ever relaxed at the table with your family while enjoying each other's company for 30-60 minutes? Then you have experienced what the Spanish call Sobremesa.

Have you ever looked up at the iridescent streaks of light that fall from the sky called **Moonbeams** and felt the peace and tranquility fill your body and mind? If so, then you've experienced what the Ancient Greeks called **Ataraxia**.

Have you ever had someone tell you to have a **magnifico dia**? They are using the Spanish term to wish you a magnificent day and secretly hoping you'll give or bestow that same gift upon others.

Have you ever slowed down and taken soft, deep breaths to calm yourself and clear your mind? Then you have connected to your **pranayama** or breath just like many yoga and meditation enthusiasts do.

Have you ever had a dream so amazing that you woke up feeling refreshed, excited, and thankful for the new day ahead?

I hope you have. I hope you do.

Note to Parents,

When my oldest daughter, Allison was six-years-old
she began having terrible nighttime anxiety. We did many
things to try and help her manage her very real and scary
thoughts including relaxing baths, soothing music, gratitude
lists, breathing exercises, bedtime stretches, and heartfelt prayers.
That challenging phase inspired me to sit down and write
this poem. It was what I had hoped our nights would start
looking and feeling like. Eventually, we found the right
combination of thoughts and habits to help us enjoy
bedtime again. Well rested children who feel safe
and secure to dream big dreams become
healthy, happy adults who change the world.

Danielle Atherton-Rutledge

Danielle is a married, midwest mom of three children,
Allison, Nolan, and Mia. When she became a mother in
2006 she realized very quickly that story time is the
perfect time to open your child's mind and heart and help
them make a little magic, fun memories, and morals that
will last a lifetime. Reading with her children has
blessed her with many opportunities to slow down,
connect, and count her blessings, and it has inspired her to
write her own playful poems.   She has high hopes to
encourage clever conversations and healthy habits that
will give children the confidence to find and
multiply the good in our world.

Courtney Heinzmann Kamm

Courtney studied art and graphic design at Eastern Illinois University. She married her high school sweetheart, Kyle and together they have 3 children: Miles, Nolan, Eloise and a beagle named Abe. Previously working for an outdoor magazine in editorial layout, she left the corporate world for freelance and the opportunity to be home with her children. Courtney's favorite mediums are watercolor and charcoal and has enjoyed bringing the fine art world into the functional art world. Her grandmother taught her laughing at yourself is a more enjoyable way to live life; life has taught her to have faith.

Made in the USA
Las Vegas, NV
10 December 2024

13757004R00021